Casey and the Beanstalk

Story by Paul Kropp

Art by Matt Melanson

kids'CBC

"Keep an open mind and an open heart. Don't take life too seriously — it doesn't last forever, you know. And may I remind you for the last time, keep your crayons sharp, keep your sticky tape untangled and always put the top back on your markers."

— Ernie Coombs

CBCtelevision

Text and illustrations © 2004 by the Canadian Broadcasting Corporation.

Mr. Dressup image used by agreement with the Estate of Ernie Coombs.

Casey, Finnegan, Aunt Bird and Alligator Al images used by agreement with Judith Lawrence.

Book design by Laura Brady.
Printed and bound in Canada by Friesens, Altona, Manitoba.

Library and Archives Canada Cataloguing in Publication

Kropp, Paul, 1948—
    Casey and the beanstalk / Paul Kropp ; Matt Melanson, illustrator.

ISBN 0-660-19239-X

I. Melanson, Matt, 1977— II. Canadian Broadcasting Corporation III. Title.

PS8571.R772C313 2004   jC813'.54
C2004-903881-8

CBC
PO Box 500, Station A
Toronto, Ontario M5W 1E6

Find more great Kids'CBC gear at CBCshop.ca

Casey and Finnegan had a farm.

Casey and Finnegan worked very hard on their farm, but nothing would grow. Soon they didn't have any food to eat.

They went to the market to sell the last thing they had — a cow.

Casey said, "We don't have any choice.
We have to sell the cow or
we'll be very hungry."

On the way to the market, Casey went off to get a drink of water. Finnegan had to look after the cow, all by himself.

Just then, an old peddler came along.
The peddler tried to sell Finnegan
all sorts of things, but Finnegan
had no money.

At last, the peddler offered Finnegan a bag of magic beans. "I'll trade these magic beans for your cow," the peddler said.

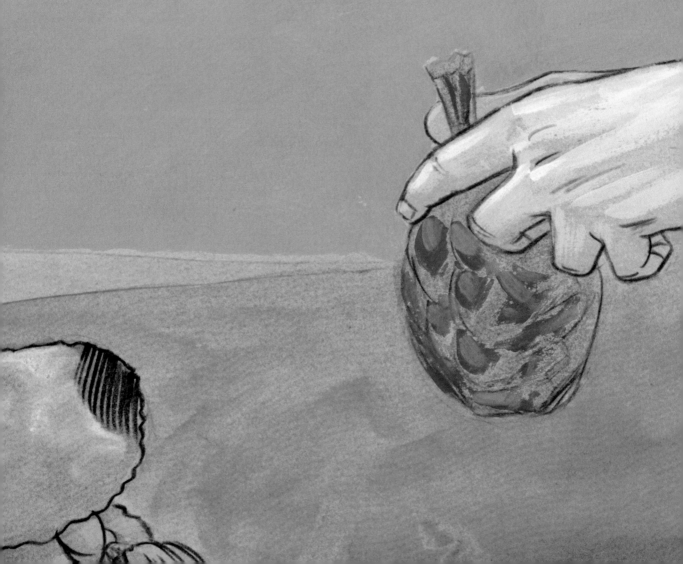

Finnegan nodded his head.

When Casey came back, he was angry. "Beans!" Casey cried. "You sold our cow for a bag of beans?"

On the way home, Finnegan whispered that the beans were really magic beans. Casey just laughed.

That night, Finnegan planted all the beans outside their house.

At midnight, something wonderful happened.
The beans began to sprout from the soil.

They began to grow,
and grow and grow!

In the morning, Casey was amazed.
"This beanstalk goes way up to
the sky!" he cried. "Let's climb it."

Finnegan nodded his head.

y and Finnegan climbed the beanstalk up, up, all the way up.

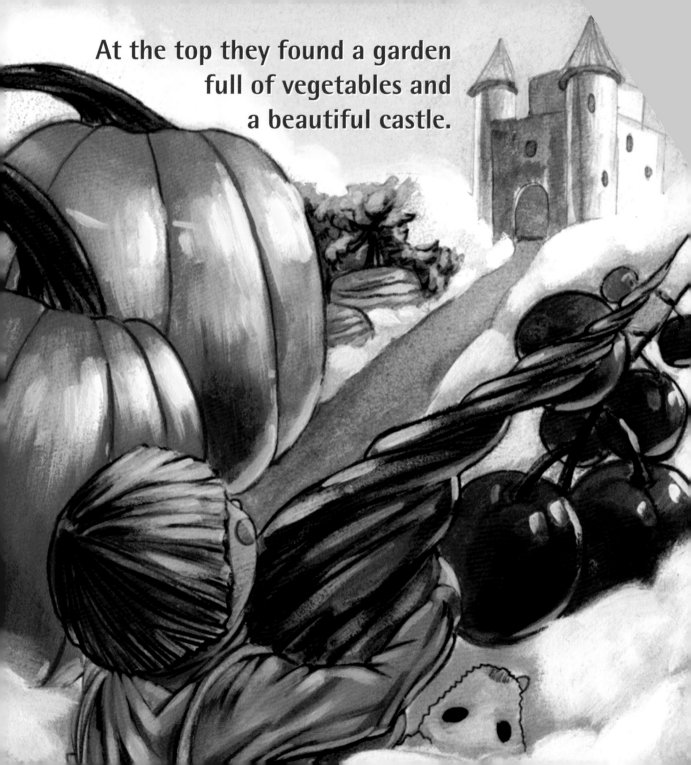

At the top they found a garden
full of vegetables and
a beautiful castle.

Inside the castle was a giant. The giant could not see or hear Casey and Finnegan.

But soon the giant smelled Casey and
Finnegan in his vegetable garden.

When the giant found them, Casey was scared. "Don't hurt us, Mr. Giant. We just climbed up to your garden because we're very, very, very hungry."

"Ho, ho, ho," said the giant
in a very deep voice.
"I am not a mean giant
like the ones in fairy stories.
I'm really quite nice,
once you get to know me."

The giant turned out
to be a very nice person indeed.
All afternoon, Casey talked, the giant laughed . . .

and Finnegan nodded his head.

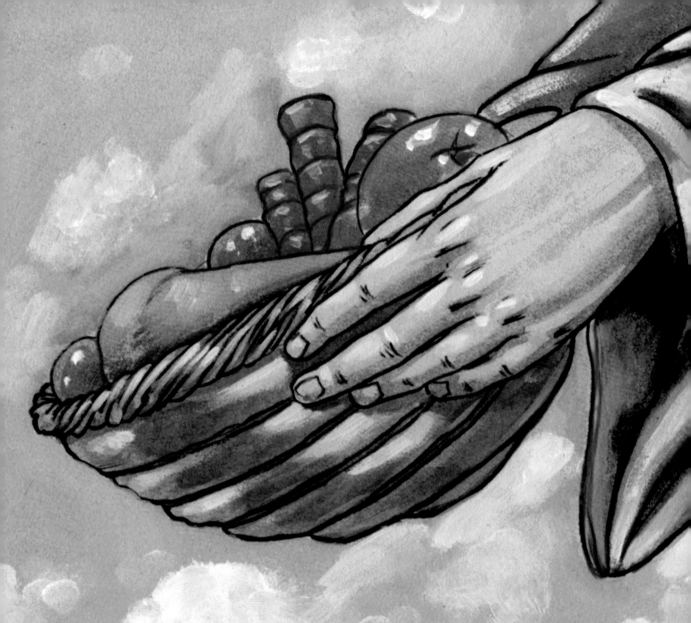

When it was time to leave, the giant gave his
new friends a very large basket of vegetables.
Casey said, "This is wonderful. Now we have food to eat."

Then Finnegan whispered a few words to Casey.

"All right," Casey said.
"We'll trade some of
these green beans
and get our cow back.
If it makes you happy."

And it did.

Time to say bye–bye now,
from Casey and Finnegan and me,
Mr. Dressup.